Gator To The Rescue

Written by Suzanne McGovern
Illustrated by Donna Bizjak

SMILE!

Pine Plains, NY 12567 • *www.GatorsGang.com*

Book design by Donna Bizjak.

Published by Hatch Ideas, Inc., P.O. Box 14, Pine Plains, NY 12567
To learn more about Gator and his pals on the farm, visit www.GatorsGang.com

Printed in Hong Kong.

ISBN-13: 978-0-9792558-2-3
ISBN-10: 0-9792558-2-1

Library of Congress Control Number: 2009906286

For Emmitt, who's happy to lead if you let him. – Suzanne

For Lily. – Donna

Gator and Milo
were swatting at flies
in the meadow together,
enjoying the weather,
when Gator thought he heard a small cry:

Gator asked Milo, "Did you hear a sound –
a small frightened yelp?
I think someone needs help!
You go get the gang while I look around."

Gator looked down in the grass
and up in the trees...

...behind rocks, in the clover,
carefully looking all over,
'til he found, well, you wouldn't believe...

"Pete!
What on earth happened to you?"

"Oooowww,"
groaned Pete with a sad turtle frown.
"I was searching for snacks
and tumbled onto my back.
Now the whole world looks
upside down!"

Just then Milo galloped back into view
with Lou taking a ride,
Nate and Marcy right behind –
all quite sure they'd know what to do.

"That's good," said Gator,
"because Pete's really stuck.
He's flipped upside down.
His feet are waving around.
And he can't get himself right-side-up."

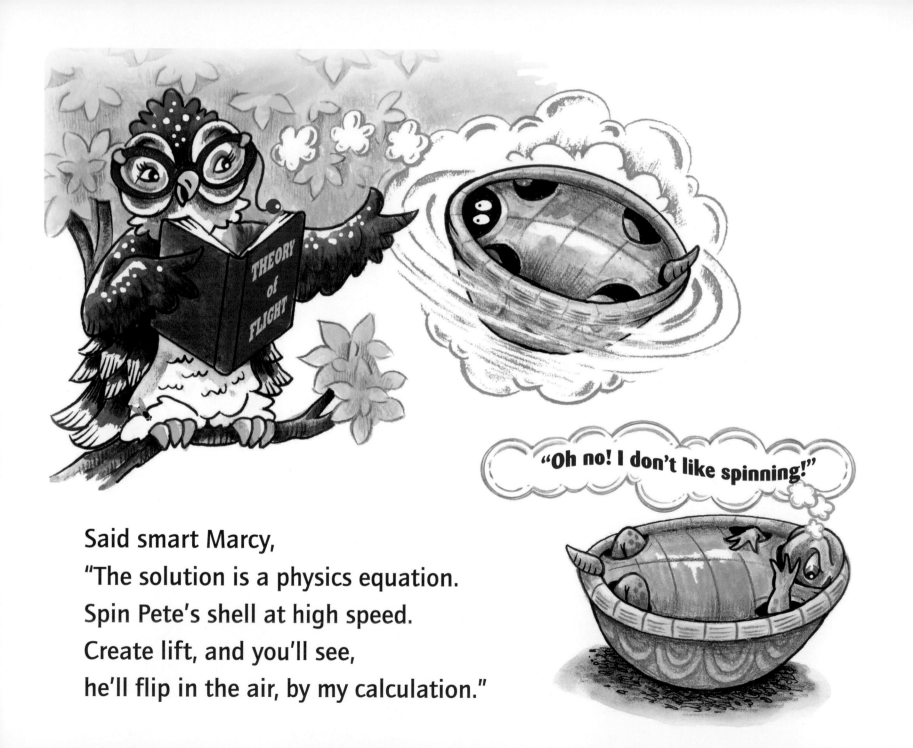

Said smart Marcy,
"The solution is a physics equation.
Spin Pete's shell at high speed.
Create lift, and you'll see,
he'll flip in the air, by my calculation."

"I know how to fix it,"
said bossy mouse, Lou.
"Pete will flip without fail
if you twist hard on his tail.
I'll supervise – that's what I like to do."

Cheered ladybug Lucy
in a voice small and sweet:
"Let's shake the leaves in the trees
and create a strong breeze.
That will blow Pete over onto his feet!"

"Oh no!
Don't stop trying!"

Grumpy skunk Nate
was in no mood to be nice.
"This is Pete's mess, no doubt,
so let him sort it out.
Why bother trying?
That's my advice."

Said Gator,
"I won't leave you, Pete. I will stay.
If we think a bit and refuse to quit,
we're sure to find a way."

First,
thought Gator,
I must cheer up Pete.
So he looked right in Pete's eyes,
then smiled super-size.
And his curled lip...

...flipped Pete...

...onto his feet.

That made the gang laugh –
Pete most of all –
knowing that when he's in trouble
and needs help on the double,
he's got a special buddy to call.

"Gator to the rescue!"

The End